THE BROKEN FIDDLESTICK

John Smith

THE BROKEN FIDDLESTICK

Illustrated by David A. Goddard

Longman Young Books

LONGMAN GROUP LIMITED LONDON
Associated companies, branches and representatives
throughout the world

First published 1971
Printed by Les Presses Saint-Augustin s.a. Brugge,
Belgium

ISBN o 582 15326 3

When the gypsy woman knocked at the back door Benjamin was in his room playing the violin. More than anything else he wanted to play it properly, but how difficult it was! When he heard the knock he put the violin down and went to the door.

The woman standing on the doorstep was dark and swarthy. A wicker basket hung over her right arm.

"Buy some pegs from Dora," she said when Benjamin opened the door. "Buy some pegs and some heather for luck, young master."

"There's nobody here but me," said Benjamin, "and I don't want anything, thank you."

The woman looked at him with her strange dark eyes. "Give Dora threepence then. It'll bring you good luck."

"I'm afraid I can't," said Benjamin. "I haven't any money." He wished she would go away and let him get back to his violin.

Before she could speak again, Benjamin heard a shout and at the bottom of the garden he saw a curious sight. At first he thought it was a boy leaping and jumping about like a clown. But when the figure straightened up Benjamin saw that he was a dwarf. Behind him stood a heavy, surly man.

The woman turned and began to walk down the path. As she reached the two men he heard her say, "There's no one there but a mean gorgio boy who won't buy even so much as a piece of lucky heather. Come, Cheko. Come, Seth. We'd best be getting back."

As they turned away Benjamin felt a sudden twinge of unease. He closed the door and climbed the stairs. Back in his room he crossed to the window and looked out. The three gypsies were walking down the road. In the distance he could see a thin feather of smoke from their camp. As he turned back to his violin Benjamin had a strange feeling that he had not seen the last of these curious visitors.

Sure enough he ran into them
again the very next afternoon. It
was high summer and the country-
side was ablaze with gold.
Sometimes, during the holidays,
Benjamin would take his violin
out into the near woods to a quiet
secret place he knew and prac-
tise there. In this remote part of
the country he rarely saw any
strangers and the few local people
were used to him by now. As he
was about to turn off the road to
cut across the fields to the woods
he met the gypsies. They must have
been watching him approach for,
as he stepped on to the grass, they
startled him by appearing suddenly
from behind the hedge. The surly
man walked up to him while the
dwarf jumped about in a grotesque
manner.

The tall man said, "Well, if it
isn't that mean gorgio boy who
wouldn't give our Dora threepence."

"That gorgio boy who wouldn't
give Dora threepence," echoed
the dwarf.

8

"Now that was mean of him, Cheko. Wasn't it mean of him, eh, Cheko?"

"That it was, Seth; mean and nasty I think," said the dwarf, and laughed.

"But I hadn't got any money to give her," said Benjamin. "Anyway, I don't see why I should. Why don't you leave me alone?"

"Leave me alone, leave me alone." laughed Cheko, jumping up and down in his curious way.

"Yes, leave him alone," said a stern voice from behind Benjamin, and immediately the two gypsies ran away across the fields.

Turning round Benjamin saw that the words had come from a dark, handsome man who was standing in the middle of the road together with a younger man and a girl who was holding a flute in her hand. They looked at him curiously.

The man said, "Don't let that Tarbath family worry you, son. They give us gypsies a bad name, with their begging and their dirty ways."

"A woman came trying to sell me pegs and things," said Benjamin. "I think she must be their mother."

The young man said, "They're an unpleasant family, the Tarbaths. They've rested their caravan down in the field yonder, but you just keep out of their way, youngster, that's the best."

"I will," said Benjamin, "thank you," and he walked swiftly away. How lucky, he thought, that they had come up just then. They were gypsies too, of course, but they seemed very different from the dwarf and his family.

In the evening on his way home he saw them again. The girl was sitting on the step of a beautiful caravan that was drawn up in the corner of a field. The paint was bright and gleaming and the camp site all about it was spick and span. From inside Benjamin could hear the sound of a violin being played. How rich it sounded! The young man came from behind the caravan and nodded as Benjamin went by.

When he got near to the field where the Tarbaths' caravan was he quickened his pace, but fortunately there was nobody about.

During the following week Benjamin saw a lot of the gypsies. Often the dwarf would pass him on the road and occasionally he caught sight of Dora and her husband. They always seemed to be shouting at each other among the litter that surrounded their caravan. But it was the other family who quite by accident were to involve him in the most extraordinary adventure of his life and who were to introduce him to the magic fiddlestick.

✑✑✑

Benjamin had often heard sounds of music coming from the caravan. Sometimes it was a single violin, sometimes he would hear singing or the sound of the flute. But the music had never been as beautiful as on the evening that was to mark the beginning, almost, of a new life. He had taken his violin to his favourite place in the woods, and it was late in the evening when he started on his way home. From quite a long way off he could hear the usual sounds of the gypsy music, but as Benjamin drew nearer to the caravan the music grew more and more vivid and beautiful. It seemed as if the whole world, the long dry grass, the straggling brambles, the trees soft against the dusky sky, the faint moon that curled like a silver fish in a frail net of clouds, was caught up and enchanted by the magic of the sound. Softly he tiptoed to the side of the caravan and stretched up as high as he could to peer through the window. But he couldn't quite reach. An old bucket, lying between the wheels, caught his eye and upending it he climbed carefully on to it and peeped through a wide gap in the gaily decorated curtains.

Then everything seemed to happen at once. There was a sudden flurry of movement and the banging of a door. In an instant Benjamin found himself clasped in two arms that felt like iron. The bucket went clattering away from under his feet and then he was lying on the floor inside the caravan. The young, handsome man was standing fiercely above him, breathing hard. He looked down at Benjamin.

"Spying," he snarled. "Spying in at the window."

The little room was very quiet.

Benjamin, pulling his violin case to him, looked up. "No," he said. "No," and suddenly he didn't seem afraid anymore. "I wasn't," he stammered. "It was because . . . because . . ."

The man towering over him said loudly, "Standing on a bucket, peeking in at the window. What's that, boyo, if that's not spying?"

Before Benjamin could reply the beautiful girl who had been playing the flute called out, "Let him speak, Jerzy. Let him say what he has to say. Look, he has a violin."

The older man, who held his own violin like a child against his chest, nodded.

Slowly Benjamin stood up and looked round at the stern faces which, even so, seemed to be kind.

"I'm sorry, sir. I didn't mean to spy. But it was the music, you see. I heard the music and. . . ."

How could he explain the strange feeling that had come over him. It would seem stupid. But then he knew it could not seem foolish to these people. "It was the music, like—like magic, and it drew me to the caravan. I just wanted to listen."

He was aware that the tall, regal man was half-smiling to himself and the dark woman, who must be the mother, was somehow stretching herself out toward him.

As if it was somebody else speaking, he heard his own voice say, "No, not to listen. I wanted to be part of it. The music seemed to be a part of me and I wanted to be a part of it." He stopped, frightened of something he could not quite understand.

The girl with the flute came and stood by him. Looking up at the tall man she said, "Father, look, he has a violin. He is like us."

Solemnly, then, without speaking, the tall man stretched out his hand and took Benjamin's violin case. Laying his own violin aside, he snapped open the fasteners and taking out violin and bow, he handed them to Benjamin. "If you are one of us," his voice was deep and caressing, "then you must prove it. You must play, my little gorgio, you must play."

The room seemed very quiet. Out of the corner of his eye Benjamin saw the flute girl and she was smiling at him as if to say "You can do it; show us that you can play." But how could he? He

could only squeak and wail and groan, he couldn't make music like the big man standing in front of him.

He tucked the violin under his chin and raised the bow. His fingers seemed like sausages. The tune that crept off the strings was thin and feeble. Benjamin nearly wept with shame and despair.

"I can't, I can't," he said, "but I want to. I want to play like you, because *you* know what music is."

The father smiled again and said gently, "If you want to, you shall. But what you need is my magic fiddlestick. That will play for you as you've never played before." He held out the bow to Benjamin.

The girl smiled at him. "Take it, it is magic. It will play for you."

Benjamin hesitated. How foolish. A magic fiddlestick. But when he raised the bow it was as if a new energy and courage flowed along his arms. He drew the bow across the strings and slowly, as if indeed by magic, he began to play and it *did* seem different. The music seemed to grow like a tree in the room.

"You see, you see," laughed the girl, "he can play. He is one of us." And then they were all laughing and clapping their hands. Even the rather fierce young man who had snatched him from the window was smiling and nodding his approval.

But now it was growing dark outside and Benjamin knew he must be hurrying home. Gravely, they all said goodnight to him. First Jerzy the young man, then the dark, handsome girl Jessie who was his wife, and Zenka the mother who bent and kissed him, and the beautiful young flute girl, Alina, who seemed to want to hold him there with her eyes and, last of all, the father whose name was Gregori. As he said goodnight, he held Benjamin's hand. "Come again next week. And I will give you some more lessons with my magic fiddlestick." Benjamin could hardly believe his good luck. He ran all the way home

and the stars that evening seemed brighter than he'd ever seen them before.

One evening, nearly a month later, Benjamin left the house at the usual time for another violin lesson from Gregori. As he passed the place where the Tarbath family rested he quickened his pace, but stole a look across the hedge as he went by. There seemed to be a lot of activity going on and Tarbath and his wife Dora were shouting even louder at each other as they carried bundles to and fro. Of Cheko and Seth there was no sign and Benjamin breathed a sigh of relief. In a few moments, round the bend, he would see again the sight that never failed to give him a strange thrill of pleasure: the gaily painted caravan of his new friends standing in its peaceful little encampment with a low fire burning close by and, perhaps, the happy figure of Alina waiting for him at the door. But this evening when he got there everything was different.

Where the beautiful caravan had been there was a desolate empty space and signs of a fight and a fire. The field which had always been so fresh and tidy was strewn with rubbish and bits of charred wood. But of Gregori and his family there was not a trace. What could have happened? Where had they gone? Why had they not warned Benjamin that they were leaving?

He began to kick among the debris half sadly, half savagely. Suddenly a familiar object caught his eye. It was the magic fiddlestick. Benjamin bent down and carefully removed it from the rubbish.

He knew then that Gregori had not left of his own accord, for he would surely not have left willingly without his precious bow.

Suddenly, Benjamin felt a sharp blow in the small of his back and before he could turn round the horrible dwarf Cheko was jumping and grimacing all round him. A little further off he could see the silent threatening figure of Seth.

Cheko bounded up and thrust his face at Benjamin: "Yah, yah, you gorgio. Where's your fine friends now then, eh? Gone off! Gone off and left you, have they? Ah, that they have. We seen to that, the Tarbaths seen to that all right. They don't come so high and mighty over us nor they don't and not know it. We seen 'em off this land for good and all, and we'll see you off, too, you snooping gorgio. Cheko and Seth, we knows how to deal with them and with your sort too, ain't that so, Seth?"

Benjamin felt very frightened in front of this strange violently gesticulating figure. "Go away," he said, knowing how weak he sounded. "Go away; it's nothing to do with you."

Cheko threw back his ugly face and laughed out loud, "Go away, he says, the stupid gorgio says go away. Oh, Seth, Seth, shall we go away then and leave the poor little boy to hisself?"

Seth came up at a run. "We're going away, boy. We're going, can't you see?" And sure enough Benjamin saw that the Tarbaths' caravan was pulling out on to the road with Tarbath himself tugging at the horse's head and his wife Dora walking behind, urging him on.

Seth was saying, "We Tarbaths come and go when we will. The Gregoris, they go where we drive them, nor they don't come back, neither." His dirty hand shot out and before Benjamin could stop him he had snatched the fiddlestick from his grasp and was waving it in

the air. "Nor they don't leave no presents behind them for their snivelling gorgio friends, neither, eh, Cheko?"

"That they don't," snarled Cheko, and, as Benjamin leaped forward to retrieve the stick, he gave him a stinging blow with the back of his hand that sent Benjamin staggering amongst the rubble.

"Oh don't hurt him, the poor baby," laughed Seth.

"No, we mustn't hurt the poor boy, must we?" laughed Cheko, kicking out at Benjamin with his boot and catching him an agonizing hack on his shin. As the tears rushed into his eyes, Benjamin heard the harsh voice of Tarbath calling from the road, "Cheko, Seth. Come. We're off." Before he could stop them Benjamin saw them turn and start to lurch across the field. As they reached the road Cheko turned, took the fiddlestick from his brother's hand and waved it high in the air in a taunting gesture.

Benjamin ran stumbling toward them, his leg still throbbing from Cheko's brutal kick. But what was the use; he could not fight against them.

As he watched them rattle off down the road, the evening seemed to grow dismal around him. Gregori had gone, and the beautiful Alina, and something else which seemed almost worse was lost, perhaps forever, in the gathering darkness . . . the magic fiddlestick.

Benjamin could not sleep. His head seemed to be twice its usual size—a great hot balloon of worry and despair. As the birds outside the window began to scrub at the darkness with their gravelly little morning songs he got up. He knew what he must do. He must go and find his friends the gypsies. But first he must get back the magic fiddlestick.

Quickly he gathered up a few things that he thought he might need on his journey; then he unlocked the tin box where he kept his savings and, so as not to lose it, wrapped his money up in a handkerchief and put it in his pocket. Picking up his violin he went down the stairs and out by the back door.

Benjamin knew that it might take a long time to find the gypsies, but he was confident that he would reach them eventually. They would be likely to steer clear of any big cities, though they might sometimes visit large market towns where they would try to sell their wares or where Dora would try to tell fortunes or beg money for the babies she didn't have. Besides, they would surely travel slowly and might even rest for a day or two in some likely spot which would give Benjamin a chance to catch up with them. People would surely tell him if they had seen any caravans on the road.

He was not afraid of being alone, and at night he was confident of being able to find somewhere to sleep, in a barn, or an outhouse to a farm. Besides, the summer weather was hot and dry. Now, as the sun began to come up and the hedges and ditches around him started to buzz and quiver into their green busy lives, he shrugged away the gloom that seemed to hang on him like a heavy overcoat. His journey was a serious task, but it was also a bold adventure and he was determined to pursue it bravely.

By the time he reached the first village people were just starting to open up their shops. He went into a little shop and bought a pie.

"Have you seen any gypsies going by?" he asked the girl behind the counter.

"No, I aint seen no gypsies," she replied, handing him his change. "What for do you be looking for them, then? Have they gone and left you behind?"

"It doesn't matter," said Benjamin, and he hurried out of the shop. Although he asked many people in the village no one had seen any gypsies.

Soon he was once again walking along the quiet country lanes. In the burning sunshine cows munched their brown and white way lazily

across the dry grassland, or sometimes a few horses would nuzzle
together in the shade of a clump of
trees at the edge of a field, flicking
up their tails to brush aside the
clouds of pestering flies. Once a
huge bull put his great head over a
gate and gazed at him as he went
by. But of Gregori and his family
or the horrible Tarbaths there was
no sign.

It was quite late in the evening
when Benjamin had his first piece
of luck. As he was passing a barn a
farmer with a horse and cart
turned out of the yard just in front
of him.

"Gypos?" The man reigned in
his horse and looked down at the
boy. "Gypos? Aye, there's been a
fair lot of the beggars on the road
just across them hills yonder. I
seen a good lot of them yesterday,
and a family today was trying to
sell me some pegs." He slapped
his thigh and laughed. "Pegs for
me. That's a good 'un. Nasty lot
they was too. I seen them afore,
that lot, that I have, with that

snivelling woman and that dirty little dwarf. Bring a bad name on gypos that kind do, to be sure."

Benjamin was so excited he could hardly keep still. "Dwarf?" he shouted. "Was there a dwarf with them? Oh please, tell me, where were they?"

Slowly the farmer climbed down from his cart and looked curiously at the boy standing there in the gathering dusk. "Now, you're up to something, me lad," he said, "I can see that. And with a fiddle too."

Benjamin said, "I've got to find the gypsies, see. It's very important. I've just got to find them. I've just got to. You must help me."

The big farmer scratched his head. "Now look here, me lad. It's late, too late for a young boy like you to be chasing round the country-side looking for gypos. You better come along of me and tell me all about it. And I'll get my missis to make us both some tea and perhaps some bacon and eggs. How about that?"

For a moment, Benjamin hesitated. It was certainly getting late and he was worn out with all his walking. He would need somewhere to sleep and, besides, Tarbath and Seth and Cheko would be stopping for the night too, so he wouldn't be losing any time.

"Right then," said the farmer. "Hop up, and we'll be indoors in next to no time and you can tell me all about it."

Benjamin climbed up into the cart and, as they set out along the road, he began to tell the farmer, who seemed to be very sensible and kind, all that had happened and why he was looking for the gypsies.

The farmer's wife was a jolly, welcoming person and soon had a meal ready for them as the farmer had promised. She was worried at first because Benjamin was travelling by himself and without any belongings, but her husband said, "Now, Ivy, you let the boy be. He can look after himself for sure, I can tell that. He can sleep here for

the night and in the morning I'll take him up the old road across the hills, that'll put him on his way."

His wife Ivy nodded. "All right, Jack, if you say so. Anyway there's no time for arguing about that now. If those cows are to be milked at dawn it's time for bed."

"Aye, that it be," agreed Jack. "First, though, don't you think you ought to play us something on your fiddle? Just for your supper like?"

Benjamin went red as he stammered, "I can't properly play, you know. Not yet. I mean not like Gregori; besides I haven't got the magic fiddlestick, you see. . . ."

"Now come on, young Benjamin, none of that talk now," broke in Jack. "You can try. You just do your best and that'll be good enough for us. One tune will do before we all turn in."

So Benjamin tucked his fiddle under his chin and nervously began to play a simple tune which didn't sound too bad after all.

"There, that was right pretty. Weren't it Jack?" beamed Ivy, when he had finished.

"Right pretty indeed. I shall dream of that music, that I shall. Well, off to bed now, all of us."

In his strange bed, in the attic that smelled of apples and hay, Benjamin fell asleep almost at once, exhausted by his long day's journey. But, as he did so, he thought how much better he would have played using Gregori's magic fiddlestick. One day, when he'd got it back, as he knew he would, he would bring Gregori to visit this kind farmer and his wife, and the gypsy would play a tune that would make them all dance. It was a promise.

The next morning, so early that the moon still floated like a ghost in the summer sky, Benjamin got up and helped the farmer with his cows. Then Ivy called them into the farmhouse where the three of them ate a good hearty breakfast in the still drowsy kitchen. Gradually the world began to wake up around them and soon it was time to leave. Farmer Jack harnessed his horse to the cart and drove Benjamin along the old track over the hills. When they reached a main road leading away to a fair sized town that could just be seen stretching along the horizon, the farmer set him down.

"There you are, my lad. There's your way. Them gypos won't stop again this side of the town, but they'll go round by the country ways and my guess is they'll camp down in the valley on the other side, by the big meadow at the bend of the river. If you take this road straight through the town you'll cut out a lot of hard walking and save time. And good luck to you. Come back and see us again with that there fiddle of yours one of these days."

28

"Oh I will, sir, I will," said Benjamin. "You've been very kind to me. Thank you very much." He watched until the farmer had disappeared back along the road then, turning his face toward the town, he started off once more on his search for the gypsies and the magic fiddlestick. But when he thought of the gypsies it was only the girl Alina who seemed to stand in front of him, encouraging him with her dark eyes as she had that first evening in the caravan.

It was a long way to the town and it seemed even longer and more wearisome going through after the bright freshness of the country morning. Around noon Benjamin went into a shop and bought himself a pork pie and a bag of apples, thinking he would go into a park and eat his lunch there, but on the way he came across a gang of workmen digging the road. They were just breaking off for their lunch. They must have come in from all parts of the town, thought Benjamin, and if anyone had seen the gypsies it would be them.

"Sure and what would you be wanting to find the gypsies for, me boy," said a tall sweating Irishman with a handkerchief tied over his head. "And for why should I be telling you now if I seen them or not, tell me that, young 'un?"

"Because it's very important that I find them," said Benjamin, looking very serious indeed.

"And for why is it so important then?" laughed the Irishman. "What's so important that a boy like you should be looking so worried about it at all?"

"Because I have to find the magic fiddlestick and give it back to Gregori because it was stolen from him, that's why."

"Oh-ho! Magic fiddlestick is it?" said the man, putting his spade down against a pile of stones. "Well now, begorrah, and there's a fine thing as I've never heard before." He pointed to the bag in Benjamin's

hand. "Now might that be your lunch you've got in there, me boy? For I'm suggesting you sit down here with Pat and tell him all about this stolen fiddlestick that's magic and all that. And perhaps you'll honour me by taking a mug of tea at the same time."

So once again Benjamin related his story. When he had finished, the man, Pat, called out to the men, "Now listen here, lads, this young scamp here is looking for some plaguey gypos what have stolen away his magic fiddlestick to be sure. Now has any of youse seen any of the thieving rogues about these parts?"

"And what will he give us, then, if we tell him?" called out a dark, thin man from the back. "What's it worth to you, nipper, if we help you to find them?"

Did the man know where they were? Benjamin couldn't be sure whether his leg was being pulled or not. "I can't give you anything," he said. "I haven't got much money you see. I couldn't afford to pay."

"Pay? Pay?" laughed Pat, and the dark man joined in. "No, but you could play, me beauty, you could play us a tune on your fiddle and that's for sure."

"That's right," said the dark man, "music while we work. You play us a tune on your fiddle and perhaps I'll tell you how to get to them gypos you're looking for."

So once again Benjamin put his violin under his chin and, although it wasn't much of a performance, the men seemed to be delighted. Even a few passers-by stopped to stare at this young boy as he played a violin to a group of workmen mending the road.

"Well," said Pat, "and it's quite a fiddler you are to be sure and well deserving of your luck. Not quite the fiddler of Dooney, but good enough. Now then, Paddy, if you know anything of these gypos you just tell the lad like you promised."

The thin, dark man came over and put his hands on Benjamin's shoulders. Yes, he had seen the gypsies. He thought they were off to a big horse fair that was being held in a few days' time outside a small market town not so many miles away. He'd seen some of them heading for the meadows by the river bend where they'd likely stop for the night, just as Farmer Jack had supposed. Carefully, so that Benjamin would remember it exactly, he explained how best to get to the place. "But you take care on yerself, me boy," he warned. "There's some in that lot I wouldn't trust as far as I could throw an elephant. Not that lot with the dwarf I wouldn't, no how!"

"Cheko?" exclaimed Benjamin. "That's Cheko. He's the one who's got it. He's got the fiddlestick."

"Well, you just watch yourself with that one, boyo," said the dark man.

"I will," replied Benjamin. "Don't you worry, I will. He's a dirty fighting thief."

"Well now, lads," called out Pat, standing up and stretching his arms. "Time as we was getting this here earth up out of this hole for the worthy citizens to have their lovely drains repaired." He turned to Benjamin. "And bully for you, me boyo. Good luck with your gypos and with your fiddlestick."

⟨≈≈≈⟩

It was not until late in the afternoon that Benjamin caught his first sight of the gypsies, but his excitement was tempered with disappointment when he realized that this family was neither Gregoris nor Tarbaths. It was a small, dumpy grey caravan with a figure of a cockerel painted in bright colours on the door and it was standing on a

scrubby patch of ground not far from the roadside. Behind it Benjamin could see that a fire had been lit and that a large, black cauldron was hanging over it. As he walked by, a thin, brown dog ran out and barked at him and a small boy carrying a pile of sticks stopped and stared for a long time without blinking. He was certain that he must soon catch up with the Tarbaths, but what of Gregori and Alina? No one had mentioned seeing them. Perhaps they were miles away in a different part of the country altogether. But Benjamin felt certain that if he could retrieve the magic fiddlestick it would lead him back to its rightful owner.

As if the thought of the fiddlestick had conjured him up out of the ground Benjamin was astonished to see the dwarf Cheko not more than fifty yards in front of him. He seemed to appear from nowhere and immediately the air was splintered with his raucous shouting. Then, lurching clumsily, he ran across the field calling out, "Seth, Seth." Benjamin trembled, but he felt certain that the dwarf had not seen him. He waited until the stumbling figure was out of sight, then slowly began to walk in the same direction.

When he got to the place where the dwarf had appeared, he saw that a deep rift had been cut diagonally across the field. It was this that had hidden the dwarf from view.

Now that Benjamin was so close to his goal he knew he must be very careful. Once any of the Tarbath family caught sight of him he knew he would stand little chance of reclaiming the fiddlestick. He sat down on the edge of the rift. Slowly he began to eat his last apple and to think out a plan.

First he decided that he should go no further until it began to get dark. Then he would go carefully in the direction Cheko had taken until he located their caravan. But where would they have hidden the bow? They would not have thrown it away, he was sure of that. How would he be able to get into the caravan and look for it without being seen? Well, first he must find out where they were camped.

It was already quite dark when he saw them. The caravan was pulled up under some trees not far from the river. A fire was blazing a

little way off and the ground was strewn with the dirt and clutter that always surrounded the Tarbaths. Benjamin could hear Dora's thin whining voice calling out something or other and the harsh grating voice of Tarbath himself answering her.

Taking great care not to make any noise, Benjamin crept towards the caravan until he was quite close. His heart was beating very fast as he crouched down behind a tangle of blackberry bushes just at the edge of the clearing. It seemed hours before Tarbath came stamping up from the river and began calling to the woman to make ready with the supper. A chill wind was blowing across the water through the reeds and Benjamin began to shiver as he huddled down in the gloom.

Then Dora came lumbering down the steps of the caravan. She was dressed in the same dragging skirt and torn filthy yellow apron. She shuffled over to the fire calling out as she went. "Come on then,

35

man, if you want to eat. Seth, Cheko, you lazy varmints, you bring some more wood for the fire too, or you'll get nothing."

There was a shout from a little way off and Cheko came bounding into the clearing followed by the surly figure of Seth and a strange, squat man whom Benjamin had not seen before. He was carrying what looked like a set of bagpipes. Seth flung a bundle of dry sticks down by the fire just as Tarbath himself stepped down from the caravan knotting a bright red handkerchief round his throat. Benjamin could see his swarthy brooding face in the glow from the fire. Dora started to ladle out food for them from the pot on the fire and the smell from it made Benjamin realize how hungry he was.

What a noise they made! Cheko's raucous laughter and Seth's growling replies to Tarbath's questions seemed to grate on the summer air. Dora was laughing too and they were passing round a bottle which Benjamin knew must be filled with some strong country wine. It was that which was making them heady.

Now, thought Benjamin, was his chance. He couldn't see whether the door of the caravan was open or not, but if he was ever going to get inside to look for the magic fiddlestick it would be when the whole family were together having a meal. Holding his violin tightly to his chest he stood up, trembling as he heard the twigs crackling under his feet. He was just about to move into the clearing when Cheko suddenly sprang up and, with a shout, ran towards him.

Benjamin froze. What could he do? He would stand no chance against the five of them. But suddenly Cheko swerved and ran up the steps of the caravan; obviously he had not seen Benjamin after all. But what a narrow escape! A few seconds later and he would have discovered the boy inside searching for the bow.

As abruptly as he had dashed in, Cheko now leapt down from the caravan and, miracle of miracles, in one hand he held a squat little concertina and in the other some sort of bulbous stringed instrument, together with what could only be the magic fiddlestick. Benjamin could scarcely stop himself from crying out.

Cheko bounded back to the fire, where the others had now finished their supper, and handed the concertina to Tarbath who started to play a strange melancholy tune. Then, Cheko began to play. As he drew the bow across the strings a hideous screeching sound filled the air. But soon Benjamin could hear that a harsh savage tune was coming from the instrument. The strange man stood up and began to accompany them on his crude bagpipes.

Benjamin heard Seth shout something to Cheko and then he snatched the instrument and the bow and had begun to play. The music was growing wilder and wilder, and all at once Cheko jumped up and began to leap round the fire in a grotesque dance while Dora clapped her hands in a fierce rhythm. Faster and faster Cheko danced as the music swelled and quickened. Then spinning round and round like a black hairy top, he fell against Seth's legs and together they went sprawling on the ground amid the laughter of Tarbath and Dora and the shouts and curses of Seth. The violin jerked out of his hands and, as his body hit the ground, the magic fiddlestick flew from his grasp and fell a little way off, its polished wood gleaming redly in the glow from the guttering fire. Cheko began to laugh in a hard, choking manner as Seth struggled to his feet, but neither of them seemed bothered about the violin or the bow. Seth was swearing horrible oaths. Then Tarbath closed his concertina and stood up. "Now that's enough of that, it's late. Seth, stop that swearing. Cheko, get up and help Dora with the dishes. We're turning in, do you hear, and I want no argument from anybody." The heavy man walked over to the caravan. At the top of the steps he turned and called out, "Ten minutes and I expect you all in bed."

Benjamin could hardly restrain his tears. Once they had all gone into the caravan and taken their belongings, he'd never be able to get the fiddlestick and now every moment he was getting colder and colder.

Cursing and grumbling the woman and the two younger men started to gather up the pots and pans. The strange gypsy muttered, "Goodnight," and lumbered drunkenly off into the darkness, his bagpipes wailing eerily under the trees.

Benjamin watched as Cheko picked up the violin and moved towards the caravan. Then he could hardly believe his eyes for the dwarf had made no attempt to look for the fiddlestick which still lay on the ground where it had fallen. Cheko and Seth were both moving unsteadily. Benjamin guessed they were both pretty drunk with the wine.

"Oh please, please," he prayed under his breath, "please let them forget all about it." With a last look out across the fire, Dora, still

38

grumbling at the men slammed the door of the caravan. And there, not more than twenty yards away from Benjamin lay the magic fiddlestick. Surely they would remember it? Any minute now the door would re-open and that horrid dwarf would rush out and pick it up.

For Benjamin it was now or never. Gathering up his courage and taking a deep breath, not caring how much noise he made, he leaped out of the bushes and ran across the clearing as fast as he could. As he bent down to snatch up the bow he heard the door of the caravan crash open and a babble of voices all shouting at once. He heard Tarbath calling out, "Who's there? Stop thief!" But, without looking back, Benjamin ran on and on through the heavy darkness until he could hear no more sound.

At last he fell exhausted under some trees. He was trembling all over, but as he lay there a wonderful glow seemed to spread through his whole body, for in his hand he held the magic fiddlestick.

It was scarcely light when Benjamin woke the following morning. His body ached with cold and cramp, but nothing seemed to matter now that the fiddlestick was once more in his possession.

Picking bits of leaves and twigs off his clothes and out of his tousled hair he stood up and stretched himself. He knew he must move on as quickly as possible for fear that the Tarbaths would start looking for the intruder of the night before.

He made his way down to the river and washed his face and hands. Although the weather was warm the water seemed icy at that hour in the morning. But as he began to walk along the river bank and the light grew stronger he felt happy and relaxed. This was the life the gypsies led and Benjamin knew it was a good and happy one. All about him the birds were singing. From the river bank he saw a water-vole slip into the stream and disappear under the surface and once a king-fisher flashed through the rising mist under the willows. The country-side seemed to be dusted with a thin powder of glittering salt as the low sun flashed across it.

Soon Benjamin was back on the road again and it was not long before he reached the outskirts of the market town where the horse fair was to be held. He still had some money left so he went into a café and ordered a large plate of sausages, eggs and chips and tea with a lot of sugar. After he had eaten his breakfast he felt much better.

When he left the café he realized that the most difficult part of his journey now lay before him. Although people would easily remember seeing a gypsy family with a dwarf like Cheko, how could he describe to them Gregori and Jerzy and Alina, except by saying how good and kind they were and that they loved to play their music. Besides, if they had been attacked and driven off by the Tarbaths, they might not even be among these gypsies assembling round the town for the fair.

The little town began to grow busy with market life and in the hustle and bustle Benjamin soon found himself, almost against his will, caught up in the excitement and activity. It was market day and all the streets were crowded with people.

It was when he was walking among the colourful stalls in the old market square that it happened. Out of the dense, jostling crowd of shoppers he suddenly heard a high excited voice calling his name, "Benjamin! Benjamin!" Then, as he looked about anxiously, trying to see where the voice was coming from, he heard again, "Benjamin. Please stop! Oh please, please stop! Benjamin, it's Alina."

There was a flurry among the people all around him and out of the agitation Alina ran, her dark hair flying, her brown arms stretched out to grasp him.

"Alina, Alina. It's you. It's really you!" Benjamin could scarcely contain himself for joy as Alina flung her arms around him and buried her face in his jacket.

"Oh, Benjamin. I knew you would find us. I just knew you would. Only Gregori said you couldn't because we were going such a long way away. But *I* was right, because here you are." Alina paused, breathless with excitement. Then more quietly, she said, "But of course you may not be looking for us at all. Why should you be?"

"But I am. Of course I am!" shouted Benjamin. "Alina, I've walked and walked and walked trying to find you. And the fiddlestick."

"The fiddlestick?" As he spoke the word Alina's dark eyes grew round with excitement. "The fiddlestick? The magic fiddlestick? Benjamin, have you found it? Have you truly found it?"

"But of course I have," said Benjamin. "Can't you see I've got it here?" He held it out to Alina who took it with eager hands, holding it almost as if it were alive.

"Oh Benjamin. It's the most wonderful thing to have the fiddlestick back again. It's very, very important to Gregori, you know, and to me."

For a moment Benjamin felt downcast without knowing why. Then Alina reached up to him and brushed her hand against his cheek. "And so are you, Benjamin. And so are you." Benjamin blushed as he looked down at her gravely smiling face. Then she took his hand and said, "Now we must go quickly back to the camp and take the fiddlestick to my father, and you must tell us all about how you came to find it and where you have been."

They elbowed their way through the streets and out towards the green countryside where the caravans were gathering.

What a scene it was at the gypsy encampment. Benjamin felt that he had been transported into a different world. Instead of the noise and turmoil of the town they had just left, here things seemed no less bustling, but relaxed and care-free.

The people—children and men and women alike—wore all kinds of gaily coloured clothing and even the old women, who were mostly dressed in black, had bright shawls over their shoulders or vivid aprons at their waists. The caravans were drawn up in a large circle, some with the horse still between the shafts, others looking as if they had already been there for many weeks. Some of the caravans were quite small and poor and drab, but others were splendid objects, glittering with newly painted designs of scrolls and flowers. They formed a small village on wheels in the large meadow with its backcloth of woods and hills stretching up, or so it seemed, into the blue of the summer sky, made hazy and quivering by the smoke from the fires.

Benjamin spotted Gregori's caravan at once, and although it was not the most important there he thought it really did look nicer than the others. Perhaps that was because the figure of gentle Zenka was standing on the top step. But it was Jerzy and his dark, silent wife, Jessie, who ran up to him first. Jessie embraced him shyly and wordlessly, as she always did, but Jerzy spun him round with a great slap on the back that nearly winded him and caused Alina to cry out, "Jerzy, you'll kill him before we've even had time to make friends again." But Jerzy gave a hearty laugh, and said, "It'll take more than a blow like that to knock this boyo down, eh Benjamin?" Then the four of them ran hand in hand to the caravan.

All the noise seemed to stop at once when Gregori turned round and saw Benjamin standing there in the doorway. His eyes, which were as dusky as sloeberries, seemed to pierce the deepest core of Benjamin's being. He did not speak. Benjamin moved forward and, holding out his hand, said simply, "I've brought the magic fiddlestick. I had to find you to bring it back." When Gregori took the bow from him it was as if an electric charge seemed to flow out from the man and along the bow into Benjamin's arm.

Gregori said, "What you have done only you will know, and what you have done is good." Benjamin was not sure that he understood the meaning of those words, but he knew that, somehow, they were important. Then all was hubbub; the family crowded round him laughing and chattering and creating a great din in the little room of the caravan. Zenka said to them after a while, "It is time this boy had food or he will surely faint away with hunger or excitement or both. Come."

So out of the caravan they went and sat round the lazily burning fire where Zenka served them with a dish of spiced meat and vegetables

that seemed to be flavoured with all the delicious wild herbs of the countryside. When Alina shyly reached out and touched Benjamin's hand, he felt as if he had never known such contentment in his life before.

The happiness of the gathering, however, was soon shattered. As they were finishing their meal there was a shout and Seth and Cheko, who never seemed to be parted, ran up and stood pointing at them. Cheko began to dance about in his usual grotesque fashion, pouring out insults at Benjamin and calling him a "filthy spying gorgio". But Seth said, in his flat, toneless voice, that Gregori would soon know what it meant to bring a foreigner into their midst. As he finished, the surly Tarbath came towards them. Gregori stood up. "I will have no more of this, Tarbath," he said. "You are evil and have evil ways and they will destroy you utterly."

Tarbath spat in the fire. "I spit in the fire of the Gregoris and all

their house. In the circle of our camp you sit to eat with a spy, a gorgio. He will bring harm to us all through your betrayal."

Gregori said, "There is no betrayal here in Benjamin. Betrayal lies in the heart and in the soul against which we have not offended."

Seth pointed to Benjamin. "He is not one of us and he must go or we will hound him out as we have hounded you and your family through the lanes and roads of the countryside."

The words coupled with the horrible grimaces of Cheko and the towering presence of Tarbath himself drove icicles of fear through Benjamin. Perhaps it was all his fault, for it was true that he *wasn't* a gypsy nor could he ever truly be one of them. Gregori was speaking again and Benjamin marvelled at the calm authority of his words.

"Tarbath, it is true that you have hounded us and tormented us because of the black hatred in your heart, but it is not through fear that we have moved on instead of fighting you. We are people of peace and live comfortably with ourselves. Our actions are just and we are not afraid. But if you try to harm Benjamin, who is a guest at our fire, we will destroy you and all who follow your dark ways of destruction."

While Gregori was speaking Benjamin became aware of the figures of two tall elderly men standing not far off. He could tell by the gravity of their presence that they were important men in this strange community. The eldest of them, who was smoking a long white clay pipe, came forward and raised his hand. When he spoke it was in a voice of absolute authority. "Tarbath, Gregori, it is a long time and still this enmity persists between you and your families. It must stop. I summon you both, therefore, to come before me at seven this evening when we shall settle the matter." When Tarbath turned to protest he went on, "Do not speak. We will hear you at the proper time. That is all."

The imperiousness of his presence and voice brought a stillness to the group that even Cheko's lumbering movements could not break. As solemnly as these two impressive figures had come so they strode away, quickly followed by Tarbath and company. As they reached their own caravan Tarbath turned again and spat on the ground in the direction of Gregori's caravan. Benjamin said, "It's all my fault. I have brought all this trouble to you, I'm sorry."

Gregori laid his hand on Benjamin's shoulder and said, "You have brought back to us the magic fiddlestick and you have the good music in your heart. You need have no fear either for yourself or for us. Soon the matter will be put right and these disputes will be at an end."

But Benjamin could not help feeling afraid as he looked round the circle of caravans and at the men and women staring in his direction.

When Gregori returned that evening from his visit to the Elders' caravan, he would tell the family little of what had happened at the interview although they clamoured round him asking for news.

"All these matters will be resolved tomorrow," he said.

Alina caught his arm. "Can Benjamin stay?"

"For tonight he will stay with us," replied her father. "Tomorrow you shall have the answer to your question. But now, why are you all looking so worried? There is nothing so bad in this world that a little music cannot help."

It was not long before the caravan was once again glowing with music. Alina took her flute and conjured from it sounds as soft as the cooing of the doves in the woods behind them; Gregori's violin seemed more beautiful than ever before and even Jessie joined in, surprising Benjamin by singing in a low vibrant voice a dark melancholy duet with Jerzy. Then Benjamin had to play and they all said how good he was. But his happiness was curbed by a slight worry that the next day held some strange problem in store for him. When at last, tired and replete with music, they began to make ready for bed, Gregori rested his hand on Benjamin's head and said, "Sleep well, Benjamin. Your worry will not stop the sun from rising in the morning nor the wind from blowing out the candles of the night. The world moves as it will and we must move with it; but I think you need have no fear."

DAVID ALLEYNE GODDARD.

It was indeed a strange world that Benjamin saw when he woke the following day. More caravans had arrived during the night and the early morning seemed a babble of voices speaking in all kinds of different languages. Most of all Benjamin noticed how friendly these people were towards each other. He was also aware, though, he was not altogether a part of it and that made him sad. He tried to avoid Tarbath and his family, but in the afternoon as he walked among the caravans chattering excitedly to Alina, Cheko ran up and made his usual horrible grimaces, screeching out, "Yah, yah, you stupid gorgio. You'll soon be gone from here. We'll soon have you hounded out of our camp. We Romanies don't want none of you spying outsiders. Nor traitors like you Gregoris neither." He danced off, shouting as he went. "You just wait, just wait until tonight. Ezra will soon send you packing." And although Benjamin was no longer afraid of Cheko, he began to tremble. He knew that before long he would have to face an ordeal. But what could it be? Even Alina, although she laughed up at him and told him not to worry, could not remove his unease.

As the day wore on it seemed to Benjamin as if all the gypsies in the world were pouring into the meadow. Alina was getting more and more excited. "It will be lovely tonight, Benjamin. You'll see. Every year we all come together like this and there is a huge fire and we sing and dance. You've never seen anything like it."

"Will Gregori play?"

"Of course. And I shall play my flute. I'll play it specially for you, Benjamin. And you must bring your violin."

Benjamin said, "Oh, I don't think I could do that. It wouldn't be right. I don't really belong here, you see."

When he repeated this, later, in the caravan, Gregori said, "No, you can never really belong to us, Benjamin, because you are not a true gypsy, but you have shown yourself to be a true friend. As for taking your violin, that is essential. That is something you must do. Now, enough talking. It is late. We must make ourselves ready."

When Gregori and the family with Benjamin stepped out of the caravan it was already dusk. The smell of burning wood was in the air and the glow from the dancing flames of the great camp-fire at

52

the far end of the field was sending red tongues licking out among the shadows. The trees on the summer hills brooded mysteriously in the darkness; only their edges quivered in the faint halo of moonlight that drifted down from the high clouds. The great crowd of gypsies looked menacing in the flickering light.

Soon, however, Gregori and the family were settled in their rightful place and Benjamin realized that they were important people in this mysterious gathering. Not far away he could see the black threatening figure of Tarbath and the jeering faces of Cheko and Seth.

Suddenly, without any warning, a hush fell over the crowd. There was a rustle of movement as the gypsies made way for the two important men Benjamin had seen the day before. How impressive they

looked, like pictures of Old Testament prophets. All was very still as the taller of them took his long white pipe from between his lips and began to speak. He talked for a long time, then he stepped back and his companion took his place. The smoke and the heat from the fire made Benjamin drowsy and he was almost asleep when he heard the words "Tarbath" and "Gregori" spoken in a loud voice, and all around the gathered gypsies seemed to stir into excited life. He heard the tall man say, "The feud that exists between Tarbath and his people and Gregori and his people must come to an end. It is foolish and it will destroy them and it will bring disgrace and harm to the Romany world."

Gregori had risen to his feet. He spoke gravely. "It is a feud that is none of my making. I am a man of peace and wish only to be left in peace."

A few low voices murmured in approval, but they stopped as Tarbath leapt up, crying out, "He is no true Romany, nor his family. They bring shame on our world parleying with strangers. Even now in this private gathering they are harbouring a spy. They should be hounded out, together with the sneaking gorgio who is hiding in their midst."

Gregori called across to him, "It is true what you say, Tarbath, that we have a stranger with us, but he is no spy. He has faced many hardships to return to me something that was lost because of your hatred and bitterness."

As if at a sign, both the Elders, looking terrifying in the glow from the fire, raised their arms and cried loudly, "Enough."

Then the chief Elder spoke. Turning towards Gregori he commanded, "Let the gorgio boy stand up and make himself known."

Benjamin was suddenly very frightened but Gregori whispered, "Have no fear, nothing will harm you."

Benjamin rose to his feet.

The tall, grey haired man looked piercingly at him. "Boy," he said, "you know you are not one of us. Why have you come to the caravan of Gregori and his clan with your stranger's ways?"

Almost as if in a dream Benjamin heard the soft voice of Alina saying to him, "You must simply tell him the truth, Benjamin, for you have nothing to hide."

"No," thought Benjamin, "I have done nothing wrong to any of these people." But he could not find the right words. It was as if he was back again on that first night in Gregori's caravan. All he could say, haltingly, was, "I am not any kind of a spy, sir, I came ... it was ... it was all because of the music." And he began to explain how he had heard Gregori playing the violin and how he had wanted to copy him. But of the troubles with Cheko or of the magic fiddlestick he said nothing.

When he had finished there was a long silence. Then the big man spoke. "And is this true, Gregori?"

Gregori said, "It is true."

Then the Elder turned and spoke with his companion in low tones. Turning once more to Gregori, he said: "Then we command that the boy Benjamin should play for us, so that we may decide."

Benjamin was terrified. He looked at Gregori. "But I can't, I can't," he stuttered. "I am not good enough."

Gregori put his violin in Benjamin's hand and gave him his bow. "You can and you must. What is music if it is not heard?" Alina said, "Play, Benjamin, play for me. Remember you have the magic fiddle-stick."

And then Benjamin found himself standing all by himself with the great dark circle of gypsies gazing intently at him out of the shadows. Shakily he tucked his violin under his chin and raised the bow. There was a deep hush from the crowd round the fire as the notes began to rise and sing in the air. They were pure and beautiful and dancing.

Suddenly the spell was shattered. It was Cheko. He had leapt from his place and was bounding towards Benjamin, mouthing ugly words and shouting to the crowd, "It's a lie, it's a lie. He can't play. It's the magic fiddlestick. It's all Gregori's witchcraft and sorcery. It is the fiddlestick, the fiddlestick itself that has the power." And before Benjamin could stop him he snatched the bow from his grasp. He raised it high in the air and then brought it down across his knee, snapping it in two pieces.

Benjamin was horrified and the watching crowd shifted uneasily. He stooped down, picked up the broken bow and ran to Gregori. "It's broken, it's broken," he cried, almost in tears. "The magic fiddlestick is broken and it's all my fault." Then he saw that Gregori was smiling. He took the bow from the boy's hand.

"Do not fret, young Benjamin," he said. "There is no such thing as a magic fiddlestick. The magic is in yourself, the magic of music, the magic of truth, the magic of love." He handed Benjamin another bow. "Here is your own fiddlestick," he said. "You must play with that now. You do not need any magic to help you, but see, I will bless it

with my own." Gently he touched Benjamin's bow with the rich brown wood of the broken stick. "Now," he said, "go and play."

At that moment, all Benjamin's doubts and fears fell away. Taking his own bow and violin he stepped back into the centre of the firelight. He walked boldly to the place where Cheko was crouching and standing in front of the horrible little dwarf he began to play. The music seemed to spring from the strings, filling the summer night with dazzling sound that tingled in the air. Benjamin played as he had never played before, and against that music it seemed as if the evil of the Tarbaths was powerless. Cheko put his hands up to his face and slowly moved back to where his family were waiting.

When Benjamin stopped playing there was a great roar from the crowd. They were shouting and laughing and applauding him. He heard amid the noise the voice of the chief Elder calling out to the whole company, but he was too overcome to hear what the Elder was saying.

He felt a tug at his side and there was Alina dancing before him. "Oh Benjamin. It's all right. You can stay. You can stay. And the Tarbaths have been forbidden ever to try to molest us again." Before Benjamin could reply the whole company seemed to erupt and the firelight was filled with whirling dancing figures. Jerzy and Gregori and Jessie and dear kind Zenka were crowding round him, laughing and congratulating him on his playing.

"You see, my son," smiled Gregori, "you do not need a magic fiddlestick to help you to play."

But Benjamin was not so sure, for had not the broken bow touched his own? Perhaps it had passed on its secret power. He knew with great certainty that he would never part with his own, whether it was magic or not.

58

The following day the gipsy encampment was strangely subdued after the festival of the previous night. Now many people who had not spoken to Benjamin before nodded and smiled as he walked amongst them. But of Cheko and the Tarbaths there was no sign.

Jerzy, coming up to him, said, "The Tarbaths have taken themselves off. They will go their own ways and leave us to go ours. Now Zenka and Gregori wish to see you. They sent me to find you."

As they entered the caravan Zenka came up and kissed Benjamin, and Gregori motioned to him to sit down. Alina sat beside him taking his hand in hers and holding it tightly. It seemed a long time before Gregori finished speaking and what he said filled Benjamin with a deep joy. The caravan had grown strangely quiet.

Zenka beckoned to her family. "Come, there is much work to be done outside." As she moved away Alina reached up and kissed Benjamin lightly on the cheek.

For a long time he remained motionless in the cosy caravan. It was true what Gregori had said. Benjamin was not a true Romany, nor could he ever become one. But he was the next best thing, a true and loyal friend, almost a blood brother. He knew that these gentle people, Gregori, Zenka, Jerzy, Jessie, but above all dear laughing Alina, would always welcome him as a visitor. The door of their caravan would always be open to him.

He could hear the sounds of movement and chatter from outside and realized how true it was that the Romany life was not one of idleness. Free it certainly was, but not altogether easy. There was always work to be done, and today Benjamin would join in that work with a will.

As he opened the door of the caravan and the bright sunshine flooded in, he saw, out of the corner of his eye, something white fluttering in the sudden draught. Hanging on a nail beside the door was the broken shape of the magic fiddlestick. The white loosely hanging horsehair trembled in the breeze as if it were alive. For a moment Benjamin paused and looked at it. Perhaps it had been magic after all. Then he ran down the steps and joined Gregori and his family in their work.

Soon all was ready for the gypsies to move off. As they turned out of the meadow Benjamin felt proud to see many men from nearby caravans come up and shake Gregori by the hand. For a long time they travelled back through the same countryside that Benjamin had covered in his search for them. Then, as it was getting dusk, they turned away from the narrow country lane and entered a cart track that led under some tall mossy trees which hung like a great tangled gateway at the edge of a wood. Deeper and deeper they went into the shadows until they emerged in a clearing where the grass spread away in folds as if someone had thrown a huge green blanket on to the earth. Alina ran excitedly into the middle of the glade dragging Benjamin

with her. "Look," she cried, throwing her arms wide, "isn't it beautiful. This is our very own special place. We come here every summer. I think it is the most wonderful place in the whole world. And now you are here with us, too."

"But only for tonight," said Benjamin. "Tomorrow I must go home." Suddenly he felt sad.

"Oh, but you will come back. Lots of times. You will come back and visit us. You must."

Benjamin smiled and held her hand tightly. "Yes, of course, I'll come and visit you."

Alina said softly, "And I will come and visit you." Then she laughed and ran back with him to where the others were beginning the task of settling the caravan into position. High above, in the dark leaves of the trees that sighed and rustled like a deep green sea, the birds were already chirping their night songs. Listening to them Benjamin became aware that he was still carrying his violin. He thought again of the curious ordeal of the previous evening. Had he really played like that? Would he ever be able to play as well again?

Gregori came and laid a hand on his arm. "Come, Benjamin," he said. "I know what you are thinking. Never fear. You will play. You have the true gift and that is something that can never be taken away from you. Besides, now you have a magic fiddlestick of your own."

Benjamin looked up into the dark gentle face. "Is it magic? Is it really magic?"

"Everything in the world is magic if you want it to be. If you love it enough," said Gregori. Then together they walked up the steps of the caravan and closed the door behind them.

CINNO